THIS BOOK BELONGS TO:

Arnold

Mick Inkpen

*Hodder
Children's
Books*

A division of Hodder Headline plc

P ig arrived at Kipper's
house with his little
cousin Arnold.

'Will you look after my
little cousin for a while?'
he said.

'Hello Arnold,'
said Kipper.

Arnold stared at
Kipper and sucked
his thumb.

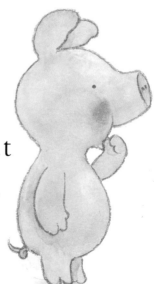

'Come on Arnold,' said Kipper.
'You can play with my toys.'
Arnold followed Kipper,
sucking his
thumb.

'Which one do you like best?'
said Kipper.
But Arnold just
looked at the toys,
and carried on
sucking his
thumb.

'Do you like Rabbit
or Big Owl?'
said Kipper.

Arnold sucked his
thumb.

'How about Slipper?
Or Sock Thing?
Or Mr Snake?' said Kipper.
Arnold took his
thumb out. . .

. . . then put it
back again.

'Hippopotamus is
good!' said Kipper.
'Look, he can squeak!'
  'Squeak! Squeak! Squeak!'
went Hippopotamus. . .

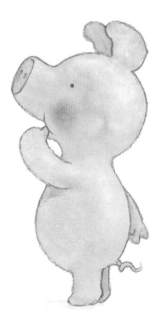

  . . .while Arnold
  sucked his
  thumb.

Suddenly Arnold STOPPED
sucking his thumb.
He went to the toybox,
and looked inside.
'Is THAT what you
like best?' said Kipper.

So Kipper made his
toybox into a
little house for Arnold,
who seemed pleased. . .

. . .and started sucking
his thumb again.

First published 1998
by Hodder Children's Books,
a division of Hodder Headline plc,
338 Euston Road, London NW1 3BH

Copyright © Mick Inkpen 1998

10 9 8 7 6 5 4 3 2 1

ISBN 0 340 71632 0

A catalogue record for this book
is available from the British Library.
The right of Mick Inkpen to be identitfied
as the author of this work
has been asserted by him.

Printed in Italy